For Pousspouss

Dial Books for Young Readers
Penguin Young Readers Group
An imprint of Penguin Random House LLC
375 Hudson Street
New York, NY 10014

Manufactured in China
ISBN 9780399186769
1 3 5 7 9 10 8 6 4 2

Design by Jasmin Rubero
Text set in Adderville ITC Std

The illustrations for this book were done with India ink and watercolor
on Moulin du Roy hot pressed paper (300 pound) and finalized with Photoshop.

DADDY HONK HONK!

by Rosalinde
Bonnet

Dial Books for Young Readers

It's the end of summer in the Arctic.

Snow will soon cover the tundra.

Everyone is enjoying the last sunny days.

Aput the little fox is watching the geese fly away.

"Oops, they forgot something!" he says, noticing an egg in the grass nearby.

He looks and sniffs.

He knocks and listens.

He shakes it and . . .

Aput goes to the lemmings.

"Would you like a baby?"

"What a little sweetheart!"
they exclaim.

But they have no room for a new baby.

Mama lemming gives Aput a tiny hat.
"A baby needs to stay warm," says Papa.
"Oh, I see. Thanks," says Aput.

Aput meets Olaf and Lily.

"Do you know much about babies?"

"Not really . . . ," answers the musk ox.

Lily is not an expert, either. But she has a suggestion. "Here, take some yummy food," she says. "A tiny shrimp like that needs to eat to become big and strong like us!"

"Thanks! Have a good hike," says Aput.

He wonders if a well-nourished baby could get as big as a musk ox.

Daddy
Crunch
Crunch!

Next they pass Nanouk doing his morning yoga.

Better not disturb him, thinks Aput.

But the baby wants to meet Nanouk.

"So noisy," grumbles Nanouk.
"Isn't it nap time?
A baby needs sleep."
"Good point," says Aput.

Daddy Roar Roar!

Aput puts the baby in a comfortable place.

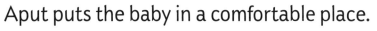

But the baby is not sleepy.

"No more honk-honk! It's nap-nap time!"

"You should rock him," suggests Granny Puffin.

But the mischievous baby definitely doesn't want to sleep.

Daddy Honk Honk!

SPLASH!

It's much more fun
to play in the water.

Daddy
Honk
Honk!

More and more friends come to play. What a ruckus!

Daddy
Splish
Splash!

Edda the whale stops the game with a big swish of her tail.

"You must always keep an eye on your baby," she says.

"Yes, phew, thanks!" Aput sighs.

"Come on, little rascal, time to go home!"

"Lets hurry.
You're chilly."

Da-da-daddy
Honk-k-k-k
Honk-k-k-k!

"Look, our house is down there."

"Here we come. The fastest
family on the tundra!"

Daddy
Zoom
Zoom!

"Welcome!"

"I will be the greatest daddy," hums Aput.

"Healthy food . . ."

"Keep warm . . ."

"We are all set for playtime and bedtime . . ."

"I think a little one like you needs a story before bed," says Aput, opening a book. Then they hear a knock at the door.

All the friends are here! What a nice surprise.
"Your baby needs a beautiful name," they say.

Under the northern lights,

everyone celebrates Aurora's birth.

Cocoa and cuddles, snacks and songs, laughs and kisses . . .

Because, above all, a baby needs love.